First published in 2013 by Tharpa Publications.

Tharpa Publications UK Office
Conishead Priory
Ulverston, Cumbria
LA12 9QQ, UK

Tharpa Publications US Office
47 Sweeney Road
Glen Spey
NY 12737, USA

Tharpa Publications is part of the
New Kadampa Tradition – International Kadampa Buddhist Union (NKT-IKBU).
Tharpa has offices around the world and Tharpa books are published in most major languages.

Text and Illustrations
© New Kadampa Tradition – International Kadampa Buddhist Union 2012

Library of Congress Control Number: 2012953546

British Library Cataloguing in Publication Data
A catalogue record for this book is available from the British Library.

ISBN: 978-1-906665-46-3 – paperback

Set in Candara by Tharpa Publications.

Printed by: CPI Group (UK) Ltd., Croydon, CR0 4YY
Paper supplied from well-managed forests and other controlled sources, and certified in accordance with the rules of the Forest Stewardship Council.

The Story of Buddha

GESHE KELSANG GYATSO

Buddhism for Children Level Two

THARPA PUBLICATIONS
UK • US • CANADA
AUSTRALIA • ASIA

Buddha was born into a royal family in 624 BC in India and his name was Prince Siddhartha.

Prince Siddhartha was a
very compassionate person.
Whenever he saw anyone who
was suffering from sickness,
he would immediately
pray for them.

Whenever he saw anyone
who was suffering from old age,
he would immediately
pray for them.

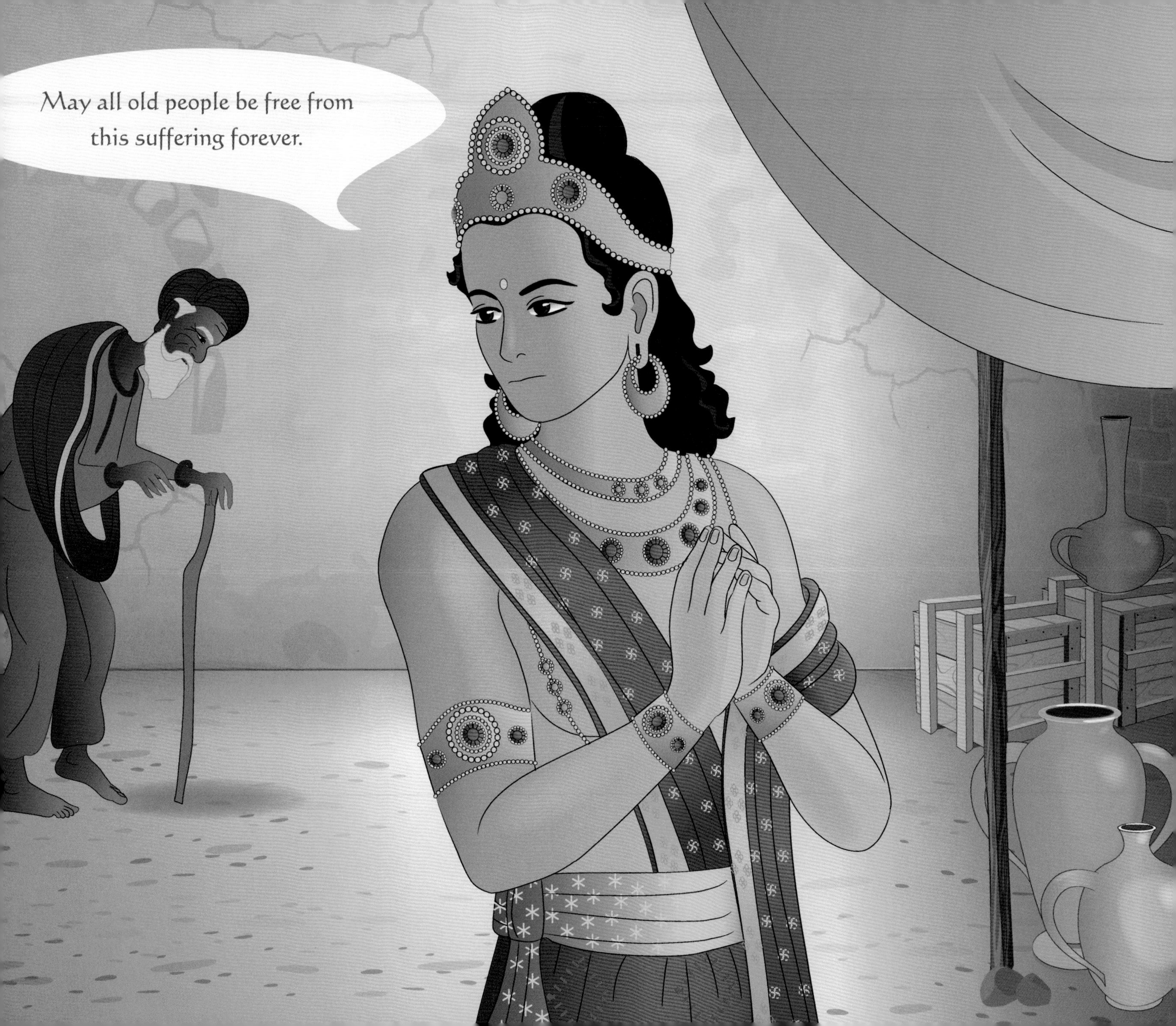
May all old people be free from this suffering forever.

Whenever he heard about
someone who had died,
he would immediately
pray for them.

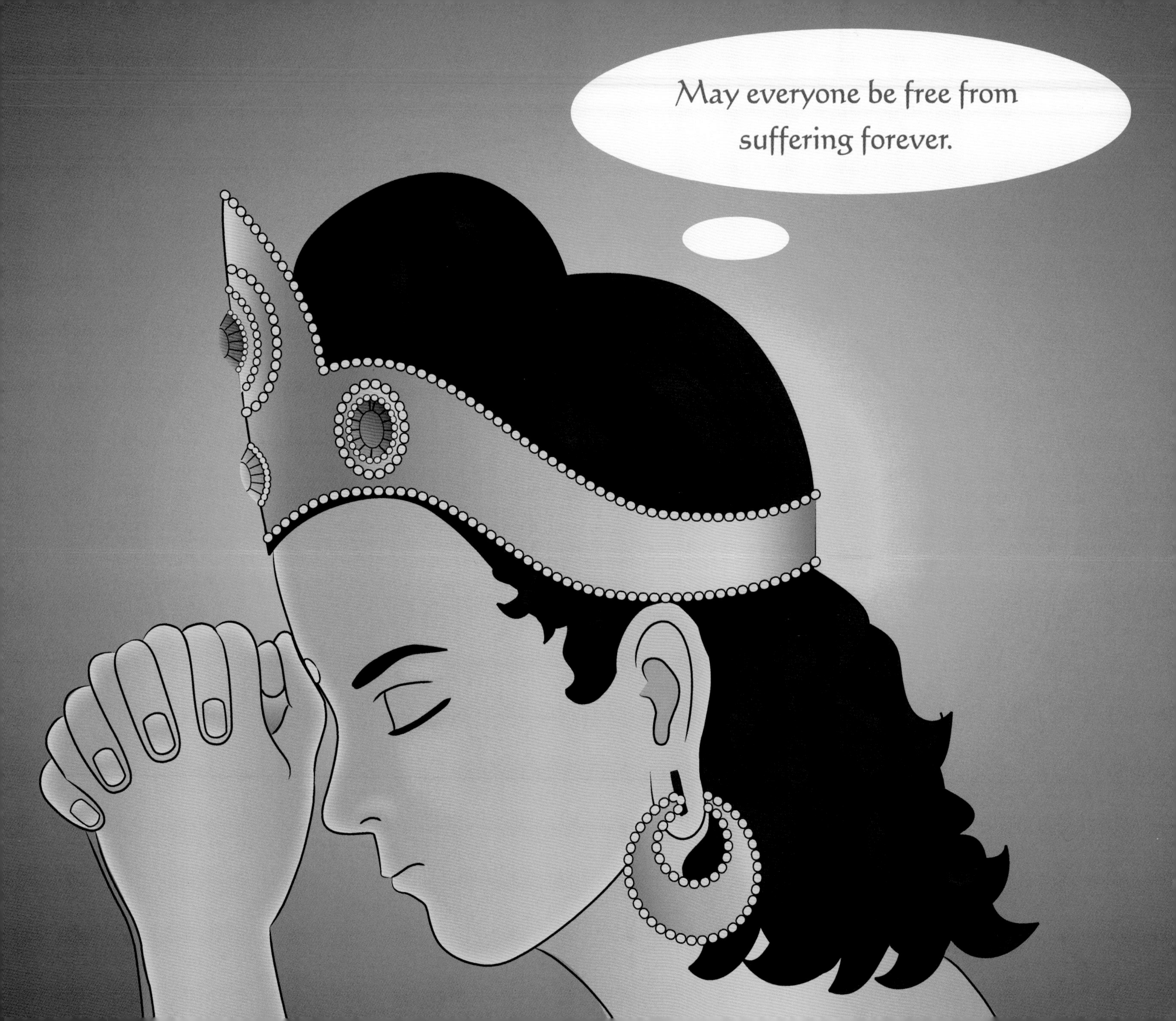
May everyone be free from
suffering forever.

Because Siddhartha's mind was completely pure he would often see many enlightened Buddhas in all directions. When he was twenty-nine years old, he had a vision of all the Buddhas of the ten directions in which they spoke to him at the same time saying,

> "*O Siddhartha, previously you promised to become a Conqueror Buddha to directly help all living beings who are trapped in the cycle of miserable lives. Now is the time for you to do this.*"

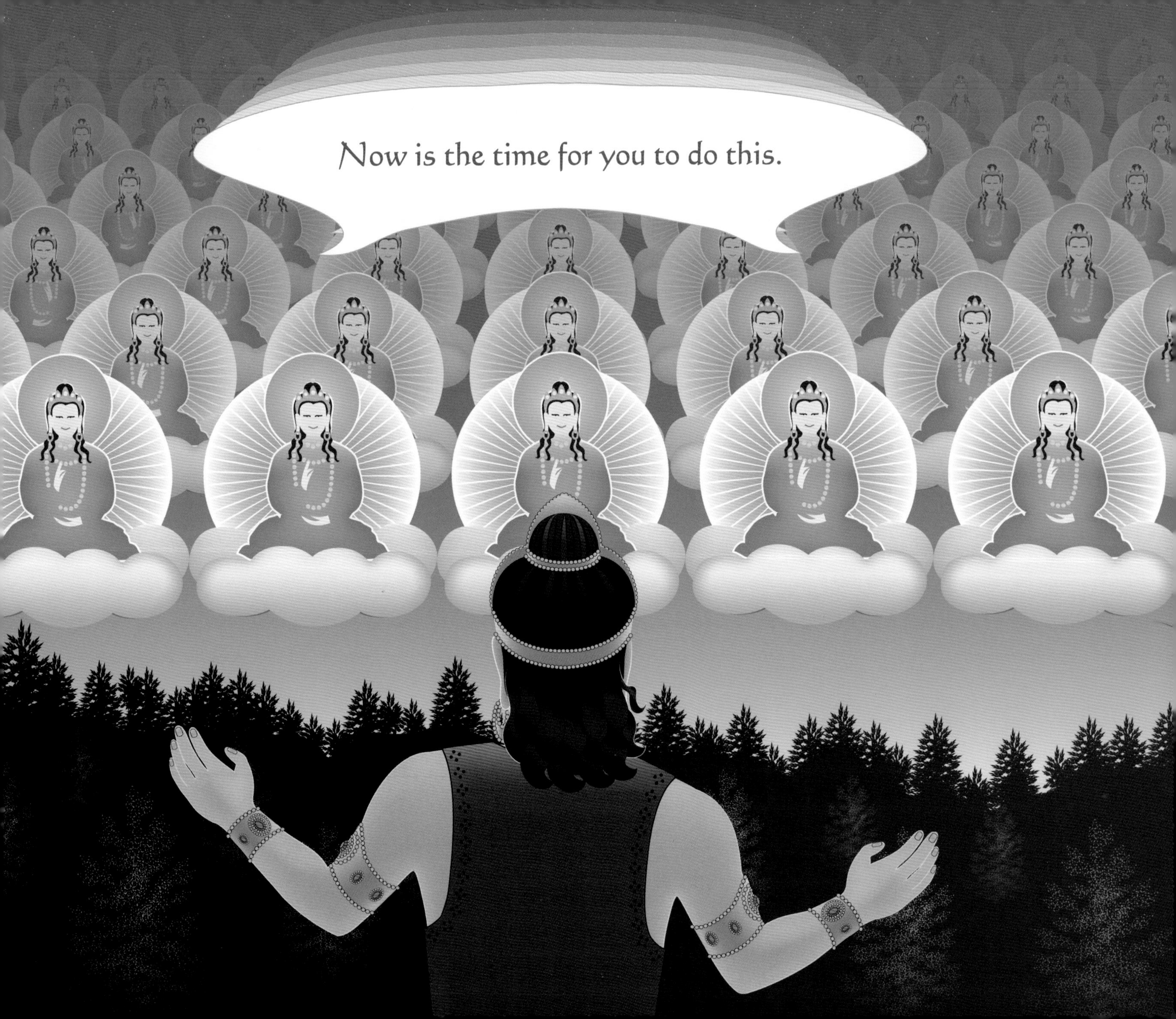
Now is the time for you to do this.

The prince immediately went to his parents and told them,

" *I wish to go to a peaceful place in the forest where I can train in deep meditation and quickly attain full enlightenment. Once I have attained enlightenment I will give happiness to all living beings and especially to you. So now I am requesting your permission to leave the palace.*"

When his parents heard this they were shocked.
The king refused to give permission saying,

" *It is impossible.*"

Prince Siddhartha said to his father,

" *Father, if you can give me freedom from the problems of anger, ignorance and jealousy forever I will stay in the palace, but if you cannot I must leave and make my human life meaningful.*"

So now I am requesting your permission to leave the palace.
It is impossible!

The king tried many ways to stop his son from leaving the palace. Hoping that the prince might change his mind, the king gathered many singers and dancers for the prince's enjoyment. To prevent the prince from secretly escaping, the king placed many guards around the palace walls.

However, the prince's determination to leave the palace could not be shaken. One night he used his miracle powers to send the guards and everyone in the palace into a deep sleep, and he then escaped from the palace with the help of a friend.

Siddhartha then went to a place near to Bodh Gaya and there he found a suitable cave for his meditation where he mainly practised a meditation called 'space-like concentration', concentrating on the ultimate truth of all phenomena. After training in this meditation for six years, he realized that he was very close to attaining full enlightenment. He then walked to Bodh Gaya where he sat beneath the Bodhi Tree in the meditation position and promised not to rise from meditation until he attained full enlightenment. In this way, he entered the space-like concentration, concentrating on the ultimate truth of all phenomena.

As night fell Devaputra spirit, the chief of all the demons in this world, tried to disturb Siddhartha's concentration by conjuring up many fearful things such as terrifying demons. Some of these were throwing spears, some were firing arrows and others were throwing rocks at him. Siddhartha however remained completely undisturbed. Through the force of his concentration the spears, arrows and rocks appeared to him as a rain of fragrant flowers. In this way, Siddhartha conquered all the demons of this world, and because of this he is now known as 'Conqueror Buddha'.

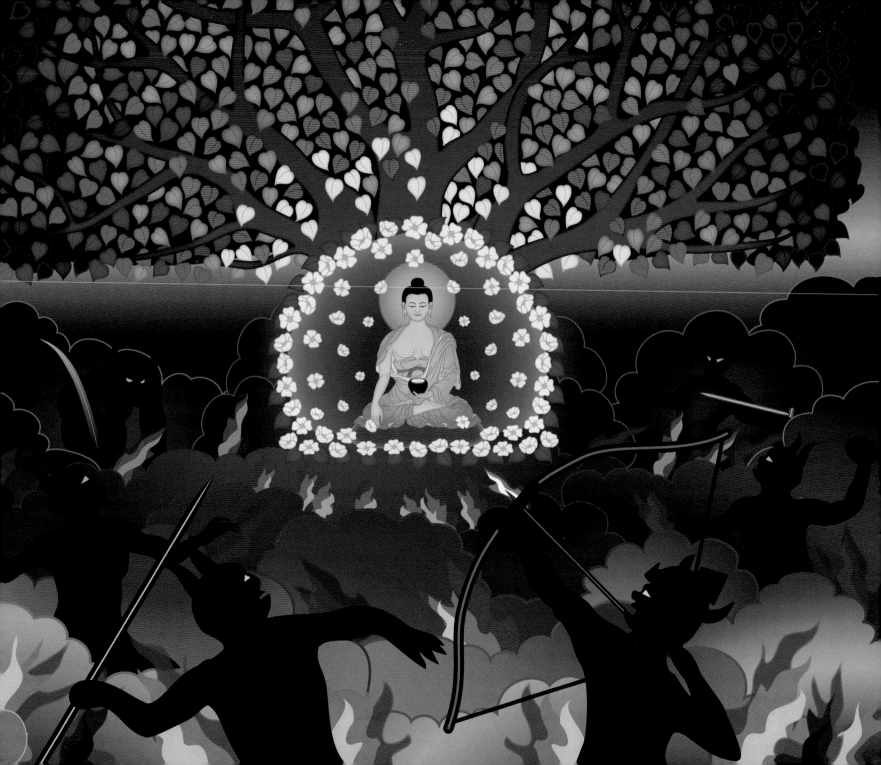

Siddhartha then continued with his meditation until dawn, when through his concentration he removed even the smallest mistaken appearance of all phenomena completely from his mind and he became a Buddha, a fully enlightened being. There is nothing that Buddha does not know. This is because he has awakened from the sleep of ignorance, and has removed all the cloud-like obstructions of mistaken appearance and obstructing thoughts from his mind. Buddha knows everything of the past, present and future directly and at the same time.

Buddha has compassion for all living beings without exception. Therefore he benefits every living being without discrimination by making various things appear throughout the universe and by blessing their minds. Gradually through meeting a Spiritual Guide like Buddha everyone will have the opportunity to attain permanent freedom from all suffering, and the supreme happiness of full enlightenment. From time to time, through receiving Buddha's blessings, everybody experiences a peaceful mind and when their minds are peaceful they are really happy, even if their external conditions are poor. Therefore, Buddha is the source of our pure happiness.

Forty-nine days after Buddha attained enlightenment the gods Brahma and Indra requested him to teach saying,

"*O Buddha, Treasure of Compassion,*

Living beings are like blind people, in constant danger of falling into the lower realms.

Other than you there is no protector in this world.

Therefore we beseech you, please rise from your meditation and turn the Wheel of Dharma."

As a result of this request Buddha gave his first teaching called 'the Four Noble Truths' in a place called Varanasi, and then on Massed Vultures Mountain he gave teachings on perfect wisdom. Because people have many different capacities for spiritual understanding and practice, out of his compassion Buddha gave teachings at many levels, just as a skilful doctor prescribes different medicines to treat different types of sick people. Buddha gave 84,000 different types of teachings and in this way his precious teachings pervaded the entire world.

If we listen to and practise Buddha's teachings continually, we can maintain a peaceful mind all the time so that we can be happy all the time. In this way, we can fulfil our own wishes as well as the wishes of all our friends.

The story of Buddha presented in this book is principally for children, but anyone who reads this story with a positive mind can develop deep faith in Buddha. Through this they will receive Buddha's blessings.

About the Author

Geshe Kelsang Gyatso, or Geshe-la as he is affectionately known by his students, is a world renowned Buddhist meditation master who has pioneered the introduction of modern Buddhism into contemporary society.

Through his personal example and his public teachings and writings he demonstrates how everyone, whether Buddhist or non-Buddhist, can learn to become wiser and more compassionate by following the advice of Buddha.

Geshe Kelsang is the founder of the International Kadampa Schools Project, which was inaugurated in September 2012 with the opening of the first International Kadampa Primary School in Derbyshire, England.

The *Buddhism for Children* series:

The **Buddhism for Children** series invites children to make a journey of self-discovery and self-improvement to help them realize their full potential.

The purpose is not to convert them to Buddhism but simply to show how everyone, Buddhist or non-Buddhist, can learn something from the teachings of Buddha.

These books address the reader in a mature fashion, using the life and teachings of Buddha as a basis for exploring many of the issues and concerns that confront children today.

Although these books are written principally for children, anyone who wants a clear explanation of the essence of Buddhism and how it applies to modern living will benefit greatly from reading them.

For more books, audio and artwork on Buddhism and Meditation visit: **www.tharpa.com**

Buddhism for Children Level 1
The Story of Angulimala

Buddhism for Children Level 2
The Story of Buddha

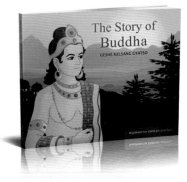

Buddhism for Children Level 3
What is Buddhism?

Buddhism for Children Level 4
What is Meditation?

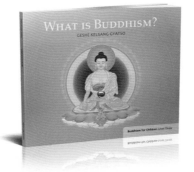